NOW IS THE TIME

The Stern Truth on Growing Your Business in Any Economy

By Marshall Stern

Printed in Victoria, BC, Canada.

ISBN: 978-1-4251-0-9764 (sc)

We at Trafford believe that it is the responsibility of us all, as both individuals and corporations, to make choices that are environmentally and socially sound. You, in turn, are supporting this responsible conduct each time you purchase a Trafford book, or make use of our publishing services. To find out how you are helping, please visit www.trafford.com/responsiblepublishing.html

Our mission is to efficiently provide the world's finest, most comprehensive book publishing service, enabling every author to experience success. To find out how to publish your book, your way, and have it available worldwide, visit us online at www.trafford.com

Trafford rev. 6/17/2009

 www.trafford.com

North America & international
toll-free: 1 888 232 4444 (USA & Canada)
phone: 250 383 6864 ✦ fax: 250 383 6804 ✦ email: info@trafford.com

The United Kingdom & Europe
phone: +44 (0)1865 487 395 ✦ local rate: 0845 230 9601
facsimile: +44 (0)1865 481 507 ✦ email: info.uk@trafford.com

10 9 8 7 6 5 4 3 2 1

CONTENTS

To my wife and kids who inspire me every day
To my mother who taught me to be honest every day.
To my late father who I think of every day.
I thank you all as I am who I am because of you.

Introduction

Okay you have done it. You have successfully started your own business. You've read the "How To" books, listened to the "How To" CD's and maybe even attended a "How To" seminar or course.

You are sitting on your new chair at your new 4'x8' fancy desk smelling the freshly painted walls in your new leased location.

Now what? Why isn't the phone ringing off the hook? Why aren't customers pounding down your door with money in hand begging to give it to you?

Did you have any idea at the time that the fancy looking 4x8 desk would take all day to build? It sure looked nice in the office furniture store.

Scenario #1

Starting a small business for many is very similar to building a pre fabricated office desk. At first glance it looks like a great idea. You see it in its full glory.

Operating, working or sitting in the showroom. You have dreamed about starting a business and now you have done it.

You're sitting at the desk in the showroom imagining yourself in the business. Hundreds and even thousands of books are available on how to start a small business.

Problem is that once you have bought the desk even though it looks great and fairly simple to put together the instructions don't quite make sense…. or worse yet, there are none!

Scenario #2

Or maybe you are an existing company that has been around for years. Like the new company you are sitting at your desk wondering how you are going to get through the months ahead. While other companies are cutting marketing budgets….**Now is The Time.**

Scenario #3

Maybe you are in an existing job or business that you are not passionate about. In fact you wake up every morning wishing you could do something else but the economy is not doing very well you are told. People are being laid off and some are losing their homes. This has to be the worst time to start something new or is it? **Now is The Time.**

Now is The Time for all of us who want more. Want to succeed in our new business. We want to grow our business from where it is now. We want to try something new. **Now is The Time** for all of us to stand up and do it. Take action.

During tough economic times most companies reduce their marketing efforts, cut budgets and lay off staff… **Now is The Time** for you to Stand Out from the others. This is the time when the truly successful business people make their move.

In the stock market Investors do not make their move and buy stocks during a bull market (when stocks are rising higher than normal). They make their move and buy stocks in a bear market (when prices are down). The best example most recently is Warren Buffet's active stock purchasing in the fall of 2008. While others were selling their stocks Buffet was purchasing them.

This book if followed can help transform your business from ordinary to extraordinary. We will cover the 4 simple steps to follow that will truly change your business. These 4 steps I refer to as the "4 Pillars of Business Growth". None of the strategies in this book are new. However the approach to executing them and combination may be. I challenge everyone who reads this to apply these principles and strategies to their business and watch the top line and more importantly the bottom line grow.

Through more than 25 years of working in and running a small business I have learned what works and what does not.

In many cases I have learned the most by what has not worked. In this book I will make 2 assumptions.

The first assumption is that you live in either The United States or Canada. The fundamentals of this book are adaptable in most business models regardless of where you live and the product or service you are providing.

Specific tactics such as marketing and advertising campaigns should be customized to the individual market it is targeting.

If you are in The U.S. and selling into Canada (or vice-versa) never assume that your selling techniques will

work in Canada just because they work in the U.S.

The second assumption is that you are a business owner, manager or in the sales field.

We are living in tougher economic times right now. Unfortunately business owners and managers look at cutting costs during these times usually in the wrong place. This book will outline some simple cost effective strategies to help your business grow in both good and not so good economic times.

Whether you have a business of your own or are in management or sales for someone else this book will change the way you look at not only your business and potential customers but your existing ones as well.

The 4 Pillars of Business Growth that you will learn about in this book are very much like plants. In order for them to grow we must take care of them and continuously nurture them. Focus on them every day and you will see your business grow regardless of the economic conditions.

Before you continue however please keep one thing in mind while you read this book:

"Life is a Journey…not a destination."
Ralph Waldo Emerson

Enjoy the journey / the process. Enjoy the challenges and mostly enjoy the ride. It will be fast and exciting if you let it be. There is no better time to lay the foundation for your business to grow. **Now is The Time.**

Congratulations on taking the first step in buying this book. Now let's get to the good stuff....**Now is The Time!**

CHAPTER 1

Focus On Yourself

"Inch by Inch, Anything is a Cinch"
- Dr. Robert Schuller

1

The first Pillar that we will focus on is ourselves. Before we can focus on specific strategies for our business growth we need to step back and figure out where we are. Take inventory of both where you are as well as your business. Once you know where you are you can define where you want to be and determine the specific strategies to get there.

ARE YOU PASSIONATE?

How passionate are you about what you do everyday? Do you wake up in the morning excited to go to work? Or do you wake up wishing you could stay in bed?

It has been found that one of the most common traits among all successful business people is that they are truly passionate about what they do. If you are one of the millions of people in North America who are not passionate then it is time that you either do something different or alter your work so that you can become more passionate. If you are a manager or business owner your passion level rubs off on your employees, just like it does with your friends and family members.

We all know someone who is passionate and infectious or the opposite and they are just "going through the motions". Which one do you want to be?

If you are not passionate at the moment and would like to become so the best advice is to reflect and ask yourself the following 2 questions:

A. What did I love to do as a child?
B. What was a very happy day for me in the past year and what was I doing?

In the area below write down the top 5 answers for each above question.

A. What did I love to do as a child?

- _____
- _____
- _____
- _____
- _____

B. What was a very happy day for me in the past year and what was I doing?

- _____
- _____
- _____
- _____
- _____

The answers to these questions may not tell you exactly what you should be doing but will guide you as to what excites you. As a business owner you may need to become more passionate. Going to work should not feel like work.

Maybe you inherited the family business and you just can't seem to get passionate about it. If this is the case do you really think that you can grow the business? You may want to consider making a list of all the tasks that you enjoy doing and the ones that you do not. For the tasks you do not enjoy doing, delegate them to someone else.

A very good resource on finding your passion is The Passion Test by Chris and Janet Attwood <u>http:/www.thepassiontest.com</u>.

"Success is not the key to happiness. Happiness is the key to success. If you love what you are doing, you will be successful."
- Herman Cain

FOCUS ON YOUR STRENGHTS

The education system in North America has taught us to focus on our weaknesses. In grade school if we got an A in Mathematics and a C in History we were told to work on our History. The problem with this theory is that maybe we are just not that great in History. Rather than work on our weakness of History we should be focussing on our strength of Mathematics.

We discussed in the last section about making a list of your likes and dislikes at work. Now do the same for your strengths and weakness. The tasks that you are weak at should be delegated to someone who is stronger in that area. Those areas that you are strong in should be what you focus your energy on.

The Pareto Principle (also know as the 80 – 20 rule) states that 80% of the effects come from 20% of the causes. You may know this in relation to your sales. That 80% of your sales comes from 20% of your clients. The same is true however to your accomplishments. With this, 80% of your results come from just 20% of your effort. In contrast 20% of your results come from 80% of your efforts. Which do you want to focus on, your 20% effort yielding 80% results or the opposite?

A great resource for focussing on your strengths is Marcus Buckingham's book *"Now Discover Your Strengths"* and *"Go Put Your Strengths To Work"*.

Take a few minutes and fill out the following two tables. Keep in mind that this is in relation to your business/career skill set.

What are my **Strengths**? (i.e. What am I good at)?

- _____
- _____
- _____
- _____
- _____

What are my **Weaknesses**? (i.e. What area am I not so good at)?

- _____
- _____
- _____
- _____
- _____

Now for all the areas you mentioned under weakness, list how these relate to you your current daily work routine. For example if you listed that you are weak at cold calling or prospecting for new clients and this is part of your job then write that down.

- _____
- _____
- _____
- _____
- _____

All of the areas that you have just listed as weakness that you do in your job you simply should not be doing. If you are a business owner or manager, delegate these tasks to someone else. If there is nobody in your organization that can do these tasks then you should review to see if this task is important enough to either outsource or to hire someone else to do.

With cold calling this is very common. Too many small business owners feel that they should be cold calling prospects. They think that this is the best if not only way to attract new business in specific target markets. If you are not good at this area or even dread doing it how effective do you think you will be? Further more you are spending all of this time and energy on something that you are not good at. Maybe rather than cold calling prospects you should focus on following up with your current customers? It may surprise you how much additional business you can actually get from your current customers. We will go into this in more detail later on.

Another example of a weakness that many small business owners and managers fall into doing is bookkeeping. I did this for the first 3 years of my business. I spent every Saturday in my office doing bookkeeping. Entering payables, writing cheques etc. Now I didn't mind the odd time doing this but every Saturday after a while got a bit tiring. Furthermore I was focussing on all of my expenses and not enough on my revenue. I then found a bookkeeper and hired her. She began coming in twice per month and in a fraction of the time had my books up to date and better yet much more organized than I ever had. I now had time to focus on my strengths. The strengths are the areas that you are good at. You may not be great but you are good and therefore you can develop them further.

Now complete the table below that will assist you in delegating away the weakness that you are currently doing in your job. The first one is an example.

Weakness	Job Function	Delegate to Who	By When
Cold Calling	Cold calling prospects	Jim (inside sales)	Today!

I should point out something about cold calling. If you are a very small business (i.e. 1 – 3 people) and there is nobody to delegate this to don't worry. We will cover more effective options to cold calling in chapter 3.

Now as you did with your weaknesses list all your strengths that you currently do or could do.

For example let's say that you are very good at writing / putting words on paper. Maybe you can put together a monthly newsletter for your clients with helpful tips about your industry or product/service.

Another example would be if you like public speaking. Contact your local chamber of commerce and see if you could speak at one of their upcoming meetings. You can also host webinars and invite your clients to attend. It can be free for them and position you as an expert in your field. Check out https://www2.gotowebinar.com.

Now make the list of how you can put your strengths to work. Don't worry if you need to develop some of these strengths further. These are strengths so it will be worth the time to focus on them.

- _____
- _____
- _____
- _____
- _____

"In examining the potential of individuals, we must focus on their strengths and not just their mistakes.
We cannot be limited by what they may have spilled in the kitchen".
-William Pollard

TAKE 100% RESPONSIBILITY

It's easy to take responsibility when you do something with a positive outcome. In sports (i.e. hockey and soccer) when you score a goal it is easy to accept the praise and admit that you are the one who scored. What happens however when you give up a goal? Do you take responsibility or do you say well the goalie should have stopped it? Many people do the latter. They want to blame others for everything that is wrong or not perfect in their life.

It almost seems safer for some to blame others. Blaming others takes them off the hook. It allows them to think that things are out of their control. Where are you in this blame game? Do you blame or take responsibility?

We all make mistakes and errors in judgement. It takes a strong person to assume responsibility. Look at your life and take 100% responsibility for where you are now. If you blame others that will get you nowhere fast.

The above is so true in our personal lives as well as our business. We may not be exactly where we want to be in our business but it is pointless to feel like a victim.

Even during tough times there is no benefit in blaming the bad economy. Where is that going to get you? Again all it does is it let's you off the hook. It takes the responsibility from your control and puts it on the economic conditions which are out of your control. But in reality if this is what you do then you really have no control. Is that what you want….no control?

Take responsibility…take action! Your life is what you make of it. Assume it… take it back it's yours.

The greatest day in your life and mine is when we take total responsibility for our attitudes. That's the day we truly grow up."
- John Maxwell

BE GRATEFUL

For some reason it is in our nature to want more and expect more. The problem with this thinking is that when we want more we sometimes lose sight and appreciation as to what we already have.

We want a bigger house, nicer car, better relationship, more customers, more money etc. Instead we should be grateful for what we do have. Look at what you have in your life that is good and be grateful for it. A good exercise is to write down 10 things that you are grateful for. This can be specific people and relationships, your health, your career or business as well as material items such as your house or car.

Make the list and then shortlist to the top 5 that you are most grateful for. Read this list every morning when you wake up.

I am grateful for:

- _____
- _____
- _____
- _____
- _____

This is the Law of Attraction. If we focus on what is bad and negative we are not showing gratitude and closing ourselves from all of the possibilities that is out there awaiting us. When we are grateful we attract more positive things to come our way.

"The essence of all beautiful art, all great art is gratitude."
- Friedrich Nietzsche

LIFELONG LEARNING

Without continually learning and wanting to learn we are limiting our abilities. By reading this book you are already open to new ideas and learning. Don't stop here.

There are many great books and audio programs available that will help you get where you want to be. Read or listen to them. Attend seminars and workshops. If you can't get to one find out if there is a tele-seminar or a webinar on this topic. The more you learn the more you will grow.

Try to do all of the above. The best method to learning is not just by reading. This is why community colleges and technical schools have become so popular over the years for employers hiring graduating students.

The following is a roadmap to how we learn. We gain knowledge by:

- 10% of what we read
- 20% of what we hear
- 30% of what we see
- 50% of what we see and hear
- 70% of what we discuss with others
- 80% of what we personally experience
- 95% of what we teach others

*"The beautiful thing about learning
is nobody can take it away from you."*
- B.B. King

CHAPTER 2

Focus On Your People

*"People who matter are most aware
that everyone else does to."*
- Malcolm S. Forbes

The second Pillar that we will focus on is "Your People". This includes Your Staff, your Business Partners and Your Network.

YOUR STAFF

You know the old saying "treat your customers like you would like to be treated"? Well that goes the same for your employees. In fact your number one and most important customer is your staff. These are the men and women that directly or indirectly communicate with the customers who purchase your products or services.

If you are unprofessional and disrespectful to your employees then how can you expect them to treat your customers?

A few ideas on ensuring that your customers (the end customer) are being treated right:

- **Be Enthusiastic:** Be energetic and show enthusiasm towards your staff and your business. If you can't get excited about your business then who can?
- **Be Respectful:** When assigning tasks be polite and professional. Don't just throw a project at someone and expect them to do it. Take the time and go over it with them. Make sure that they are comfortable with the assignment.
- **Be Professional:** This includes dressing appropriately for your position and your business. Also avoid using foul language especially in relation to a customer or project.
- **Be Helpful:** Allow your staff to come to you for assistance. Open door policies mean more to them than

you think. It also means more than simply leaving your door open.

- **Be Flexible:** If it is a slow day let your employees go home early and you hold down the fort. This may not be possible with some organizations but if you candle handle it, a little can go a long way in boosting employee morale.

- **Have Fun!** We all have to spend a majority of our waking hours at work. Make it as enjoyable as possible. The more your staff likes to be at work the more productive they will be. After work take your staff out for dinner. Go play paintball or go bowling. The main thing is to get to know your employees and allow them to bond outside of the workplace.

- **Empower:** The more you allow your staff to make decisions on their own the more they will feel like they are part of the company and making a difference. Allow them to share their ideas. Like you, they should also be encouraged to take 100% responsibility for their work and their decisions.

- **Training:** Lifelong learning is not just for you. You should allow your people to learn and grow within the industry and within your company. Send them to seminars & courses. Allow them to participate in workshops and other events that they may gain valuable training and insight. Even if the topic is not directly relevant to your company or industry it may assist your staff to grow in their position.

- **Passion Test:** You have taken the time to discover your passion level now gauge your staff's. Are they passionate about their job and about your company? We spend the majority of our waking hours at work so why not make it a great place to spend your time. Check in with your staff frequently to see how they are doing and if they need anything. The more you do the items above, the more passionate they will be about their work.

If you are a one-person company or an account representative and have no staff then use the extra time to focus on the other areas covered in this book.

List 5 ways that you can focus more on your staff starting tomorrow.

- _____
- _____
- _____
- _____
- _____

"Start with good people, lay out the rules, communicate with your employees, motivate them and reward them. If you do all those things effectively, you can't miss."
- Lee Iacocca

YOUR PARTNERS

Most business owners feel that their suppliers should look after them. This is true but it should not be a one - way street. Ensure that you have a good relationship with your suppliers because you never know when you will need them.

You may have equipment problems one day and need extra fast service or your inventory is short on a particular product and you need it fast. The better your relationship is with your supplier rep the better positioned you are for that "special" service. Depending on the industry sometimes suppliers get enquires from the end consumer and then need to refer them to one of their customers. Be that company they refer.

Review your supplier list and determine which ones you would like to build a better relationship with and then begin to grow it. Take them for lunch or golfing. Maybe you can send them a Season's Greetings card or gift.

Now make a commitment to contact these suppliers and take action. **Now is the Time!**

Supplier	Contact	Action Step	By When

Forming strategic alliances can be one of the most powerful

strategies in growing any business. The more that other businesses can help you the better. Whether they are funneling you business directly or through referrals it can be a win win situation.

In addition to suppliers, look at other businesses that you could partner with. It may be another company within your industry whom does not compete directly with you. Maybe their product offering is slightly different.

An example of this would be an off-set printer and a quick printer. The off-set printer may specialize in larger runs and orders for magazines, newspapers etc. whereby the quick printer may be better suited for business cards, letterhead and newsletters for smaller companies. The two companies are in the same industry but really don't compete with each other. However they both would get enquires that the other company may be better suited for.

Another form of strategic alliances would be for two companies that are in similar industries and target the same type of client.

An example of this would be the printers we discussed above and a graphic designer. Both go after the corporate accounts. Why not team up with them and see how you can help each other gain more business. The printer's clients may have needs for a graphic designer and of course with graphic designers much of their work is displayed through print.

List 5 current or potential partner companies that you could form strategic alliances with.

- _____
- _____
- _____
- _____
- _____

Now make a commitment to contact these potential partners and take action. **Now is the Time!**

Company	Contact	Action Step	By When

"Coming together is a beginning.
Keeping together is progress.
Working together is success."
-Henry Ford

YOUR NETWORK

Your network consists of the partners we just discussed but also those you meet through organizations and meetings. As with yourself, your staff and your partners make a plan of what you are looking for or missing in your network.

Be selective as to which business events you go to. Events cost you time and money. These are two very precious resources.

When determining if you should attend a specific event ask yourself two simple questions:

#1   Will I learn something valuable from attending?

#2   Is it beneficial for you to meet others at this event?

If you answered no for both #1 and #2 then do yourself a favor and put your time to better use. If you are not going to grow your network or knowledge then go exercise or spend time with your family.

List 5 networking organizations that may be beneficial to you. This may include Chamber of Commerce, BNI (Business Networking International), industry associations etc.

- _____
- _____
- _____
- _____
- _____

Now make a commitment to check out these Networking groups and take action. **Now is the Time!**

Network	Meets When	Action Step	By When

Now list 5 types of companies, industries or specific companies that you would like to meet and add to your network.

- _____
- _____
- _____
- _____
- _____

Now make a commitment to check out these Networking groups and take action. **Now is the Time!**

Company	Contact	Action Step	By When

CHAPTER 3

Focus On Your Customer

*"Do what you do so well that they will
want to see it again and bring their friends."*
- Walt Disney

So now you know where you are. You have turned your focus from yourself onto your staff and partners. Now is time for the third Pillar: Focus on Your Customer.

CUSTOMER COMMITMENT

One of the main strategies in growing your business is to focus on your customers. I know this may sound weird…Focus on your customers? Why would anyone want to do that?

Okay let's be serious for a moment. There is an epidemic in North America today that I call "consumer apathy". What I mean by this is the apathy that business has towards the consumer. Many say that the customer is top of mind but in reality profits are.

Take the banking industry for example. They keep adding service charge after service charge. If you think about it what the heck is "Service Charge"? Why should customers have to pay for service?

Banks are a service driven industry and rely on their customer service for keeping business. To charge for that service seems almost hypocritical.

It is time that business owners throughout North America redefine their purpose and mission. Over the past 20 years the buzz-word was "MISSION STATEMENT". You have to have a "Mission Statement". So what did organizations do? They designed a fancy paragraph that said what they wanted their customers to hear and titled it "Our Mission Statement".

You see by simply having a "Mission Statement" that spoke about their service and commitment to their customer they really didn't have to do much else. As long as they preached it did they really have to focus on it daily? We all know the answer.

Now there are some exceptions as there always is. In the retail sector many small independent specialty shops offered exceptional customer service but at a premium. Because they were small and specialized, the price for their products was higher than you would find at larger stores and department stores.

Then along came the Wal-Mart. Although they began in 1962 the major expansion came in the early to mid 90's. Wal-Mart saw this apathy and decided to rock the boat. Not only would they practice what they preached about service with a smile but they did this at the lowest prices. Now they can do this because of their size. Most of us are unable to do this and that is perfectly fine. In fact it is very fine. Do you really want to play the price game anyway?

The point here is that Wal-Mart has good customer service. Also they are very consistent in everything they do. From layout and design of their stores to employee training, the "customer experience" is the same every time.

Some may call it customer service, customer satisfaction but I prefer "Customer Commitment".

"The goal as a company is to have customer service that is not just the best, but legendary."
- Sam Walton

Every company and their dog boast that customer service

is important to them. The question is however, what kind of customer service? Good customer service or bad customer service?

Customer Commitment is just that…."COMMITMENT to the CUSTOMER plain and simple. If you build your business with this philosophy in practice your business will grow.

Books have been written, programs developed on this subject. Some call it WOWING your customer. Under-promise and over-deliver.

These are all fine but how about simply finding out what the customer wants and giving it to them in a friendly courteous manner. If you are one of those that think Wowing you customers is the way to go well it may win them over but then you need to have a system in place to consistently WOW them. Then eventually one day you don't WOW them and all of a sudden they are missing the WOW.

I am here to tell you that you don't need to WOW them. Just listen to them. Respond to them and give them what they want and if for some reason you can't, direct them to who can. You can't be everything to everyone but you can be helpful to everyone.

It is your job to ensure that you and everyone that is part of the client fulfillment in your company is Customer Committed.

From the person who answers the phone or greets your customer to those that package and deliver your products or service they all need to have the customer in mind. Greet them, be kind to them, help them, smile and say thank you. Do you say thank you for the order? Do you follow up with them?

Building a customer committed business is like building a house. You must first build the foundation. Customer Commitment is the foundation of your business. With that you can build the rest. Without that you are in for some very rough times.

Have you done any renovations to your house or business in the past few years? During the housing and renovation boom how was it finding a contractor? Better question is how was it dealing with them?

Contractors were so busy during the past few years that for many of them all that they saw was the money in their pockets. The Customer Commitment was left out. For many of these contractors this was not the case.

Did you ever try to call them after your project was done? Or even during the project when you were waiting for something to be finished.

As busy as your business may get after using the secrets in this book, do not take anything or anyone for granted. Your customer is only your customer as long as you value them. As long as you have their best interests in mind. As long as you are Customer Committed!

Build the foundation first. Ensure that everyone in your company is on board with the Customer Commitment Philosophy and then and only then should you continue on with this program. Even if you stopped here at least you have the foundation for a great business that customers will want to come back to time and time again. They may even tell others about you.

TAKE YOUR CUSTOMERS TEMPERATURE

Are your customers happy? How do you know this? Don't take it for granted. If they are happy that is great but the worst thing you can do is go out and ask unhappy customers to refer you to their friends, family members and business contacts. This can backfire for you and anger some of your customers.

Back in 1996 my wife and I booked a weekend up at a spa resort on Vancouver Island in British Columbia, Canada. Friends told us that this particular spa was very special and "a must experience". They had a great experience themselves and wanted to share that with us.

This word of mouth form of advertising is what we all strive for. Wouldn't it be great if the customers just kept flocking to us without little extra effort? It can and it will but first things first…back to my story.

Anyway we packed up our bags and headed on the ferry over the Pacific Ocean to this Spa Oasis that we heard so much about. The problem with this story is that it was a Spa yes but NOT an Oasis.

For starters this spa was undergoing renovations and the spa rooms were closed. The treatments would now be done in a very bright open room. Not what you expect from a spa.

If that wasn't bad enough I needed a spa weekend after sleeping on the horrible lumpy beds.

In any case we left a day early and went home very unsatisfied. I wrote an email to the resort expressing my displeasure with the facilities and that my back was in much worse shape since I slept on their beds.

What I had hoped was an apology and that either they would look into correcting this situation (maybe new beds) or at least a slight refund on the weekend. Instead what I received was a letter with a credit note for a future stay. I guess at least they offered that but why in the world would I go back for more of the same.

Now if they had mentioned that they were working to rectify the situation by possibly getting new beds and apologized for the inconvenience then the credit note is a nice touch and we would consider going back once they got new beds. Instead what they did was actually nothing to address the real issues, which were uncomfortable beds at their spa resort. They missed out on an opportunity make the situation right and having us recommend them to others.

So many companies miss out on these opportunities. Don't be one of them. The customer is our purpose...not our disturbance.

> *"Customers don't expect you to be perfect.*
> *They do expect you to fix things when they go wrong."*
> - Donald Porter

The first step in any referral program is taking the temperature of your customer base. If you consistently perform customer follow up then you already have a general idea on your customer satisfaction level.

If you don't do this follow up (it's a great idea if you began now) then the easiest way to begin is by calling them. Just ask them "how are we doing" or "how is our service". Open-ended questions are the best way to gather feedback. An example of this is:

1. What areas can we improve on?
2. How do we compare to other suppliers that you work with?
3. Is there anything that we can offer that we may not at this time?

Another way you can find out what your customers think about you is through a survey. Today the Internet allows us to do online surveys with a few clicks of the mouse. Check out the survey option at www.constantcontact.com. You can email out an online survey to your customers and get instant feedback. They even have a free trial period where you can try the service at no cost. Not a bad way to gain a bit of credibility with your customer base without spending a dime.

REFERRAL MARKETING

Companies around the world spend thousands and even millions of dollars in attracting new clients. Yellow page advertising, expensive direct mail campaigns even hiring a sale force all in the hopes that someone will say yes to their offer or at least be somewhat interested in the product or service. It doesn't have to be this way.

Are you tired of cold calling? Do you hate when others cold call you? If the answer is no then you are one of two kinds of people: One who lies or one who enjoys doing things the hard way. Cold calling in the US and Canada have taken a big blow with the "Do Not Call" list. The problem is that it only applies to Residential cold calling.

The challenge now more than ever is finding ways to attract new clients while still focusing on keeping our existing ones happy. After more than 14 years running my own business I finally got sick and tired of chasing new clients. Pondering the question… now do I hire a sales force?

I guess you can say it was at that time I had a "light bulb" moment. Here I was sitting on a client list of more than 4,000 companies that have used my services in the past. Many of them still do. These clients who continually use our services are happy or at least seem to be. They keep coming back for more.

I am not a stats person but I will mention a few (that means only three) in this book. Statistics show that it costs 8 to 10 times more to get a new customer than it does to keep an existing.

As I mentioned earlier I struggled after years of chasing down prospects trying to convert them to new clients. Then it hit me. What better place to start building my client base than with these repeat loyal clients. That is when I decided to start my first referral program and have never looked back. It was so successful that I kick myself at times for not thinking of it earlier.

Referral programs have been around for a long time. Very few companies however utilize them.

There are many variations of referral programs but they all have the same result. One company that I have worked with setup their referral program whereby customers who gave referrals were immediately entered into a draw with the winner getting 3 months of service for free. If that referral became a customer then the referring company received a discount on their next order.

Another variation is to simply offer a discount to all referrals. You can also have the double-ended program whereby there is an incentive for the referring company (i.e. Coupon or credit towards a future order). The referral would then get a discount on the initial order.

Whichever program you decide to go with ensure that you follow the next few steps. Without them you are just wasting your time as well as your customers.

1. Database Cleanup

Once you have ensured that your customers are overall satisfied with your company you can then proceed to the next step which is setting up the list of customers that you would like to target.

You may decide to target your entire database. If you do this be sure to delete from the mailing list any customer that you know of that is not happy. With that said however, if you have customers who are not happy you can turn the situation around and find a way to repair the relationship. In some cases however this may not be possible. Believe it or not the customer is not always right. I have seen situations before where a customer has unreasonable expectations or do not take responsibility for errors that they have made. Instead they blame the vendor (being you or me). For these types of customers they should not be included in this program.

It is at this point where you should now cleanup your database. What I mean by this is ensure the contact information and mailing address is correct. Depending on the size of your database you may choose to do this in-house or hire a temp to update the database. Either way the person who does the phone calling to update the database must be professional and easy to understand. Remember every contact with your client is a reflection on your business.

2. Get The Word Out

Okay now you are ready to put the program in place. The first step is to outline how you are going to do this. A great way to do this is both by email and snail mail.

The email method is fast and free. Those are 2 very good reasons to start there. Providing these are clients and they have given you their email address then send out a nice short email announcing the new referral program.

All you are doing in the email is informing your clients that you are introducing a referral program and they will receive more information by regular mail.   In the email you can let them know that if they know of anyone that may be able to use your product or service to pass on your name to them.

If you don't want to ask for the referral in the email that is perfectly fine. We can do that with the mail out. Or if you prefer you can wait until you actually phone them. This is the most personal approach and will yield the highest response.

Once you have your database ready and your initial "teaser email" sent out it is time to send out the letter.

A simple professional letter can be very effective. The more clever and gimmicky you get the more it will look like just another promo piece. A simple letter on professional letterhead gives your company credibility. Make the details of the program easy to understand. Begin and end the letter by thanking your client for their business and you look forward to working with them in the future. (see sample letter on next page)

Once the letter has been sent ensure that the program is in place within your company. Everyone needs to know not only how the program works but how it will be administered and managed. This all depends on the type of database or Customer Relationship Management system that you have.

The best way to get referrals is to give referrals.
Give and you shall receive!

Sample Client Letter

February 2009

Dear Customer,

As the year winds down all of us at XYZ Company are gearing up for a very exciting 2009. Before the New Year begins however I would like to introduce you to a very special program that will take effect immediately, "The XYZ Referral Program".

How it Works

If you are happy with the service that we have given you then please pass our name on to any of your contacts that may order signage from time to time. This may be a friend, family member, business associate or your own customer. When this referral makes their initial purchase with us they will receive a 15% referral discount. As a thank you we will credit your account $50 towards a future order.

Please note that if for some reason you are not completely satisfied with our service please let us know. We value our relationship with you and want to ensure that you are getting what you need and want from us.

You have my commitment that if you refer someone to us we will take excellent care of them.

If you have any questions on this new program or any immediate needs please contact us at 555-123-1234.

Sincerely,

Bob Smith

President

CHAPTER 4

Focus On Your Brand

"Make it simple. Make it memorable.
Make it inviting to look at. Make it fun to read."
- Leo Burnett

You have now Focussed on Yourself, Your People and Your Customers. The fourth and final Pillar of Your Business Growth is to Focus on Your Brand.

WHAT IS A BRAND?

According to the website Wikipedia a Brand is "a collection of symbols, experiences and associations connected with a product, a service, a person or any other artefact or entity."

Companies spend thousands and even millions of dollars on creating their brand. The problem is that during economic downturns many cut back their marketing efforts thus jeopardizing their brand. Now is the time for all of us to step into the forefront and lead the way in our marketplace.... leaving our competition behind.

There are hundreds of books on building your brand and I won't even pretend to be an expert in this area. What I do believe however is that there are a few key areas that we should all focus on in building and maintaining our brand and place in the marketplace.

BUSINESS STATIONARY

It may seem basic and I assume you already have business cards and letterhead. Ask yourself the following questions and if you answer no to any of them you should rethink your stationary.

1. Is my letterhead and business cards consistent with each other?
2. Are they professional in their appearance?
3. Do they have the proper company colors?
4. Do our business cards have the most updated information?
5. Are they double sided?

The last question in particular may have you scratching your head. Double Sided? The reason that I mention this is that you are already paying for the stock so why not pay a bit more and utilize both sides. Even if the backside only has your company logo or a list of your products and services utilize this space. Also I recommend using a quality stock. Spend a bit more for the good stuff. As they say a first impression goes along way. Ask your printer for options to help your company stand out from the others.

WEBSITE

If you don't have a website get one. Plain and simple. Websites are so inexpensive now that you can get one of the template site builder sites up and running for a few hundred dollars for the entire year.

Here are a few tips on effectively branding your website:

1. **Keep it current:** Change the content weekly if you can.
2. **Easy to Navigate:** The days of the fancy flash sites are over. Eyeballs don't want to wait for the flash intros to end. They want a simple and easy to navigate site. As in large retail stores there is a method to the madness. Products are located in certain places that will attract the most attention. The same holds true for your website.
3. **Brand Consistency:** I can't mention this too many times. It is so important that your website is consistent with the rest of your brand and marketing. Including logo, colors and message.
4. **Professional:** This may sound too simplistic or obvious but it is not. If you want to be taken seriously as a business owner or manager then make sure your site is serious. You can have fun with it but ensure that it is professional. That includes spelling and grammar which I found out the hard way a few years back.
5. **SEO:** Everyone and their dog are talking about SEO (Search Engine Optimization). This is mainly being fuelled by the companies that either specialize in SEO or the Google's and Yahoo's of the web world. Driving

traffic to your site is important but you need to weigh the cost / benefit first. SEO can be fairly expensive. How you are found on the web will be slightly determined by your target market. If your market is local then all you may need is strong keywords and metatags. Another good way of driving traffic to your site is through Google AdWords program (check out www.adwords.google.com for more information).

MARKETING / ADVERTISING

As discussed several times already, during economic downturns marketing is usually one of the first areas that companies cut back on. You may decide to reallocate your marketing dollars to other areas but try to keep them somewhere. This is your chance to really step away from your competition. Maybe you want to put your money more towards driving traffic to your website. You may want to consider expanding on your email marketing campaigns or direct mail marketing campaigns. You know your business and industry so look at all of the options. Ask yourself and others in your company the following questions:

1. How Can We Become a Leader in our Market?
2. What will it take?
3. How can we gain the competitive advantage over our competition?

SIGNAGE

Effective use of signage can not only enhance your brand but also create more awareness of your brand than traditional marketing.

THE ABC'S of Signage

Attract New Customers

Brand the Business

Create Impulse Sales

Attract New Customers

Whether it is new customers moving into a geographical area or daily traffic going by your place of business signage can attract new customers. If you have a storefront then banners and effective window signage and displays can bring in new business. Keep your signage current. If you are in retail change the signage from time to time or put up a temporary banner. People are creatures of habit and when something has been changed in front of them they will notice.

Think about your daily commute. You take the same route everyday passing by the same businesses. Have you ever noticed something different on your way to work? Maybe a new company has opened or a new sign has been installed. For ideas on how signage can benefit you and your company check out www.sandboxsigns.com and www.4pillarsofbusinessgrowth. com.

Brand the Business

Professionally done signage can take your brand to a whole new level. Have you ever noticed the golden arches or the green mermaid? If you haven't guessed I am referring of course to McDonalds and Starbucks. Both of these companies have used signage as one of their main ways of branding. Consistency again is the key. Ensure your sign company adheres to your brand identity including proper usage of your logo and its colors.

You may decide to wrap or decal your vehicles. You may align yourself with a special event such as a golf tournament or sponsor a sports team. Whatever areas you focus on utilize signage as an effective tool for enhancing your brand.

Create Impulse Sales

Signage can also generate sales that you would not normally get. POP (Point of Purchase) signage is strategically placed in retail aisles and throughout store shelves in effort to get you to buy their products.

The latest development in technology has spawned a huge growth in digital signage. Digital signage is basically the ads you seen on LCD screens everywhere you go. Elevators in office buildings have them showing the weather, stock information along with advertising. Restaurants and other establishments are now using them in their restrooms. Wal-Mart has LCD screens at every checkout and throughout the stores creating impulse sales.

Other ways to create impulse sales can be simply through banners hanging in your place of business or outside. Sandwich boards and window graphics are great for bringing customers inside. Another great product being used everywhere is floor graphics and counter graphics. The latter is used at the checkout stand and usually strategically placed where you place your money.

There are many different ways you can grow your business with signage. Check out your local sign company and ensure that they have are somewhat knowledgeable in marketing principles and not just making signs. Another great reference for the benefits of signage and how they can help you brand your business is www.signs.org.

The key with your brand is to be consistent in all of the areas that you focus on. From your business cards to your website, advertising and signage keep the message and the look and feel consistent throughout. You will be rewarded in the long run.

Summary

There is no better time to grow your business than right now. So many companies are scaling back, unsure about the future. Take advantage of this time and step up to the forefront. You owe to yourself, your people and your customers.

If you follow the 4 simple steps in this book (the 4 Pillars of Business Growth) you will be fine...actually better than fine. If you take care of your customers they will take care of you. Focus on Yourself... Focus on Your People... Focus on Your Customers... and Focus on Your Brand. **Now Really is The Time!** For more information on the 4 Pillars please visit www.4pillarsofbusinessgrowth.com

"May Your Business Grow Beyond Your Dreams
& Your Dreams Beyond Your Business!"
- Marshall Stern (Author of this book)

10 Tips To Growing Your Business

1. Be Passionate about what you do
2. Focus / Work on Your Strengths everyday
3. Be Grateful for all that is in your life
4. Take 100% Responsibility
5. Commit to Lifelong Learning
6. Focus on Your People (your staff, your partners, your network)
7. Focus on Your Customers: Be customer committed
8. Referral Marketing Programs: no more cold calling
9. Network in the right places
10. Use Effective Signage for promote your business